This
Treasure Cove Story
belongs to

_____

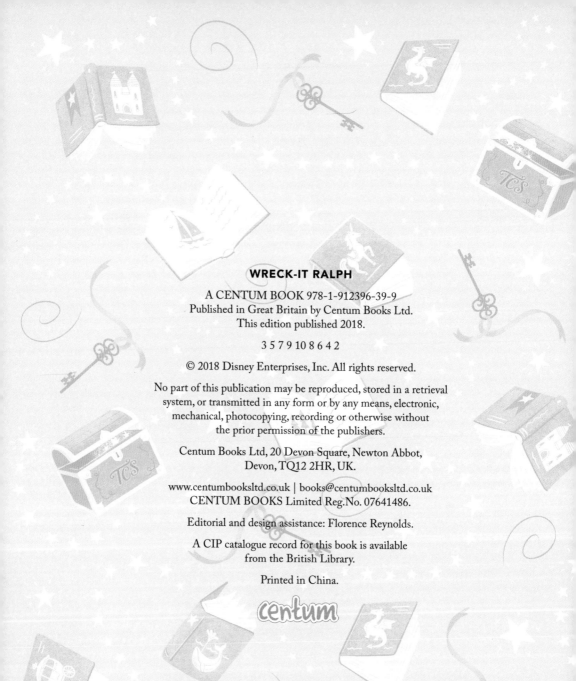

WRECK-IT RALPH

A CENTUM BOOK 978-1-912396-39-9
Published in Great Britain by Centum Books Ltd.
This edition published 2018.

3 5 7 9 10 8 6 4 2

Centum Books Ltd, 20 Devon Square, Newton Abbot,
Devon, TQ12 2HR, UK.

www.centumbooksltd.co.uk | books@centumbooksltd.co.uk
CENTUM BOOKS Limited Reg.No. 07641486.

Editorial and design assistance: Florence Reynolds.

A CIP catalogue record for this book is available
from the British Library.

Printed in China.

centum

A Treasure Cove Story

Disney
WRECK-IT RALPH

Adapted by
VICTORIA SAXON

Illustrated by
LORELAY BOVE

Designed by
TONY FEJERAN

Ralph lived in a video game. His job was to **WRECK** a building every day, *game* after *game*.

That was why
he was called the
BAD GUY.

The Nicelanders, who owned the building, threw Felix parties, made him *FANCY* cakes...

...and gave him MEDALS.

Ralph didn't get any
MEDALS.
And he didn't get invited
to any parties.
Ralph was lonely.

Ralph made a *BIG* decision.

He left his own video game and travelled to another game to search for a MEDAL.

ZOOOOOM!

Ralph thought that once he got a MEDAL he would be a GOOD guy and everyone would love him.

Ralph got his MEDAL,
but he lost it in a game
called Sugar Rush.

Then he found a little girl named Vanellope who wanted to be a racer.

She had his MEDAL! She needed it to enter the big race.

King Candy didn't want Vanellope to race.
He said Vanellope was a video game **GLITCH**.

GLITCHES were not allowed to race!

Vanellope asked Ralph to help her build
a better and faster race kart.

Ralph needed Vanellope to win back his MEDAL.

At King Candy's garage…

...Ralph and Vanellope worked together to build Vanellope's kart.

They did it!

King Candy told Ralph
that Vanellope didn't
belong in Sugar Rush.

If she raced, the video game would break.
Then she would be stuck in Sugar Rush **all alone**.

King Candy returned the
medal to Ralph. Ralph wanted
to save his friend Vanellope,
so he did what he did best
– he **WRECKED** everything.

Now Ralph had a **MEDAL** but no friend.

Ralph sadly went back home.

When he got there,
he peered out of the
video game screen and
saw the Sugar Rush
game in the arcade.

Vanellope's picture was on the game! Ralph figured out that King Candy lied. Vanellope DID belong in Sugar Rush!

Ralph went back to Sugar Rush. He discovered that Vanellope needed to cross the finish line to become a real racer. Ralph found Fix-It Felix in King Candy's dungeon! Felix had come looking for Ralph because the Nicelanders wanted him back. Their video game didn't work without... **Wreck-It Ralph!**

Ralph asked Felix
to do
what he did best.

Felix **FIXED**
Vanellope's kart!

Ralph helped Vanellope get to the race.
He realized that Vanellope was much
more important than a MEDAL.

VAA-
R-R-R
OO-OOM!

Vanellope raced
as fast as she could.

She used her
GLITCHING powers
to disappear and reappear
in front of the other racers.

Vanellope crossed the finish line!
She was a real racer at last!

Ralph went home. He saved his
game. He didn't feel bad about being
the Bad Guy anymore.

And he didn't need a MEDAL,
because now he had friends.

That was all Ralph needed
to prove he was really a good guy!

Treasure Cove Stories